THE LOCH NESS MONSTER SPOTTERS

Tony De Saulles

Orion
Children's Books

ORION CHILDREN'S BOOKS

First published in Great Britain in 2017
by Hodder and Stoughton

1 3 5 7 9 10 8 6 4 2

Text and illustrations © Tony De Saulles, 2017

The moral rights of the author and illustrator have been asserted.

A CIP catalogue record for this book
is available from the British Library.

ISBN 978 1 5101 0185 2

Printed and bound in China

The paper and board used in this book are from well-managed
forests and other responsible sources.

Orion Children's Books
An imprint of
Hachette Children's Group
Part of Hodder and Stoughton
Carmelite House
50 Victoria Embankment
London EC4Y 0DZ

An Hachette UK Company
www.hachette.co.uk

www.hachettechildrens.co.uk

THE
LOCH NESS
MONSTER
SPOTTERS

There are lots of Early Reader
stories you might enjoy.

Look at the back of the book,
or for a complete list, visit
www.orionchildrensbooks.co.uk

For Max and Jinty
from Uncle Tony and Betty

This is a bird spotter.

This is a butterfly spotter.

This is the McFee family. They are
Loch Ness Monster spotters.

Mummy McFee,

Fern McFee,

Daddy McFee,

Finley McFee,
and
Betty
McFee.

The McFees are Loch Ness Monster mad!
"We call her Nessie," says Fern. "She lives
in a big lake called Loch Ness."

The McFees wear Nessie T-shirts, Nessie hats
and Nessie badges.

They read Nessie books and watch Nessie programmes on the TV.

But the Loch Ness Monster spotting family have a problem. They have never, EVER spotted the Loch Ness Monster!

Every summer the McFees set off on holiday. They go to the same place and do the same thing every year.

"We go Loch Ness Monster spotting!"

But Finlay is tired of looking for the
Loch Ness Monster.
"We never, EVER see Nessie. I don't
think she exists!" he says.

"No Nessie? Nonsense!" says Dad.
"We just need to look for her in a
new way."
"I have just the thing," says Mum.
"A boat!"

"We have only looked for Nessie from the shore," she explains.
"Now we can explore the whole loch."

But the McFees have another problem.
There are four McFees and only three
life jackets.

"And Finlay can't swim," says Dad.
"I'll stay here and look after Betty,"
says Finlay.
But Mum and Dad are worried.

"We'll be fine. If you go in the boat and we explore the shore we will have a better chance of spotting Nessie," Finlay says.

"Well, okay, but be careful," says Mum.

"Don't forget your camera!" says Fern.

Finlay waves goodbye as the little boat
rows across the loch.

But Finlay has ideas of his own.
"Let's forget the Loch Ness Monster
and go for a walk," he says.
Finlay and Betty have a great time.

Skimming stones,

hopping over streams

and following animal tracks.

Finlay meets an old man sitting by
his caravan.

"I've been living here for twenty years,"
he says. "I look for Nessie every day."

"I don't believe in the Loch Ness
Monster," says Finlay.
"She's out there somewhere," says the
old man.

Finlay climbs a tree that
has fallen into the loch.
"I'm a pirate climbing
up to the crow's nest!"
he shouts.

"I'm on the lookout for Mum and
Dad's... booooooooooooooooooooat!

Finlay can't swim.

His rucksack is pulling him

down,

down,

down,

through the deep, dark water. Finlay
thinks he is going to drown. But then
he changes his mind.

He is going to be eaten instead.

Sharp teeth grab Finlay by the sleeve.
He is whisked away, whooshing
through the water
at great speed.

Finlay can't hold his breath any longer.

He needs to...

BREATHE!

The Loch Ness Monster has saved Finlay.
He can't believe his eyes. Nessie does exist!
Mum and Dad and Fern will be SO
excited, he thinks.

Finlay looks around. He is in a cave.
Is this Nessie's home?

He snaps some photos.

Nessie is friendly.

But then Finlay starts
to shiver and shake in
his cold, wet clothes.

Nessie blows hot air to warm
Finlay up. He puts his wet
clothes on a rock and does
a little dance in his pants.

When Finlay is dry he shares his tuna sandwiches with Nessie and they look through his Loch Ness Monster book.

Nessie has never seen a book but she enjoys looking at the pictures.

A long time ago a fisherman spotted a monster swimming in Loch Ness.

Ever since then people have been searching for the Loch Ness Monster. Everybody was excited when this photo was taken.

But it was trick. It was just the
head of a plastic sea serpent
fixed to a toy submarine!

Then Nessie footprints were
discovered on the shore of
Loch Ness.

But this was another trick.

The footprints were made with

the foot of a hippopotamus!

Would anybody find the real Nessie?

A circus owner offered a big reward for anybody who caught Nessie alive!

Scientists used machines to search for her.

Scanning machines.

Listening machines.

Even robot submarines!

But what sort of animal is Nessie? Is she a prehistoric beast that has survived from the age of the dinosaurs?

Or just a big eel,

or a seal,

or even a giant catfish?

Perhaps Nessie is just water.
Sometimes the waves on Loch
Ness look like a sea serpent.

Finlay closes his book. He's not sure what sort of creature Nessie is. He just hopes she is happy and not lonely.

There is a splash.

It's a baby Nessie!

Finlay can hear a dog barking.
Is it Betty?
The sound is coming
from a tunnel.

It's time to go home.

Finlay gives Nessie a hug
and waves goodbye as he
starts to climb the tunnel.

As he climbs he thinks about Mum and
Dad and Fern. They will be so proud when
they hear that Finlay has found Nessie.

Perhaps Finlay will appear in the newspapers or maybe they'll make a TV programme about how he discovered the Loch Ness Monster.

He will be famous and people will
come from all over the world to see
the incredible creature that lives in
the loch.

But as Finlay reaches the end of the
tunnel he starts to think about Nessie
instead of himself. How she saved his
life, warmed him up and dried his clothes.

She's not a monster. Nessie is a kind
creature living happily with her baby
in their secret underwater cave.

Finlay sees Daddy McFee rowing
the little boat back to shore.

"We haven't seen a single thing!"
Mummy McFee shouts.

When all the McFees are on dry land they light a fire and cook sausages for their supper.

"Tell us about your day, Finlay,"
says Dad. "Did you see Nessie?"

"I looked and looked but I didn't find her. I told you, there's no such thing as the Loch Ness Monster!"

What are you going to read next?

Don't miss
more monster adventures...

Learn how to stomp and stamp in **Mondays at Monster School.**

Have fun with Monstar and her furry new friend in **Monstar's Perfect Pet.**

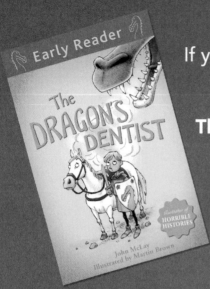

If you like **The Loch Ness Monster Spotters**, you'll also enjoy **The Dragon's Dentist**,

or find out about other mythical creatures with a **non-fiction Early Reader.**